Island Dog

Rebecca Goodale

Two Dog Press

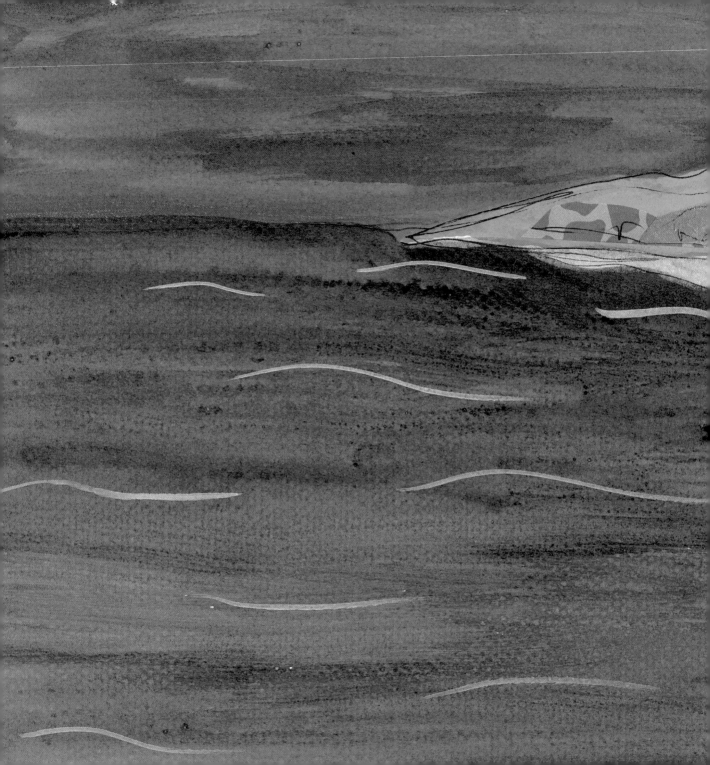

Island Dog

Rebecca Goodale

for Mom and Dad

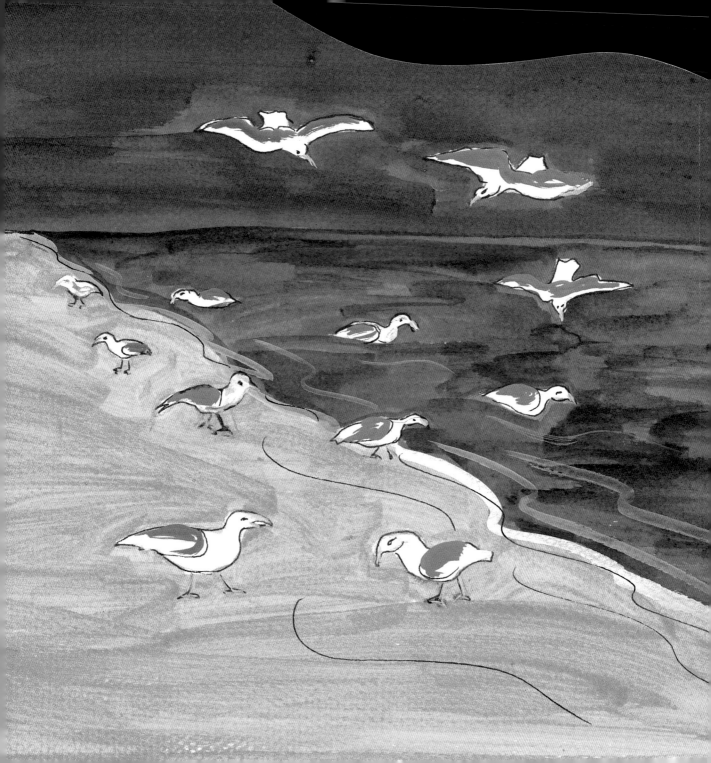

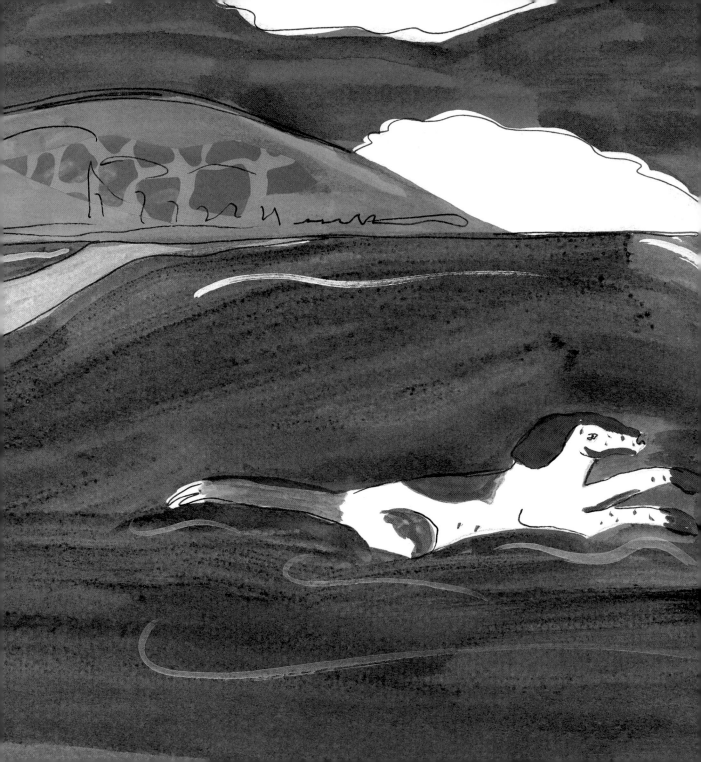

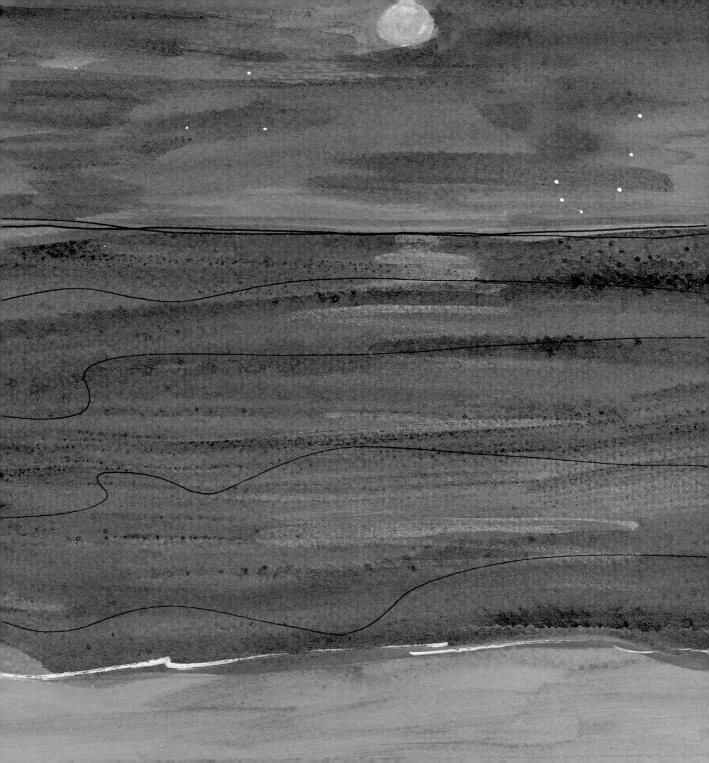

Artist Rebecca Goodale creates unique and limited-edition books, many with sculptural elements and special details influenced by her rich background in printmaking and textile design.

She received a BFA from the Memphis College of Art in Memphis, Tennessee, and did graduate work at the Cranbrook Academy of Art in Bloomfield, Michigan. In addition, she was a resident scholar for the Island Institute in Sitka, Alaska, and a recipient of the New Forms Regional Initiative Grant from the New England Foundation for the Arts.

Goodale's work is widely exhibited and is in several private and permanent collections, including the New York City Public Library, State of Hawaii, Georgia Council for the Arts, and The White House Ornament Collection. She teaches at the University of Southern Maine and lives in South Portland, Maine—where the beach in her neighborhood often has more dogs than seagulls.

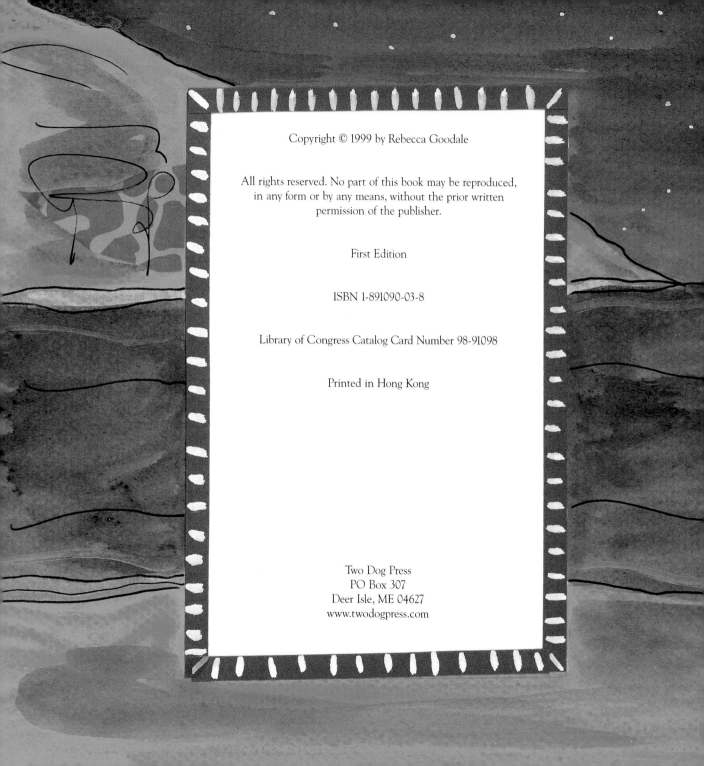

First Edition

ISBN 1-891090-03-8

Library of Congress Catalog Card Number 98-91098

Printed in Hong Kong

Two Dog Press
PO Box 307
Deer Isle, ME 04627
www.twodogpress.com